ADVENTURES OF
JABOTÍ
ON THE AMAZON

LENA F. HURLONG
ILLUSTRATED BY JOHN VERNON LORD

ABELARD-SCHUMAN
LONDON NEW YORK TORONTO

J

Hu-c.4

London	*New York*	*Toronto*
Abelard-Schuman	Abelard-Schuman	Abelard-Schuman
Limited	Limited	Canada Limited
8 King St. WC2	6 West 57th St.	1680 Midland Ave.

Printed in the United States of America

Contents

Preface

These fables, in which the Brazilian tortoise, Jabotí, is the central figure, were gathered by the author from natives living along the upper Amazon River.

In these tales, Jabotí is depicted as sluggish in his movements, not strong, and yet he is made to overcome the powerful tapir and the fierce jaguar thus proving that astuteness, intelligence, and perseverance (not to mention the sympathy of the gods) are more powerful than brute strength.

The dramatic as well as the amusing situations, and the naiveté displayed, make them delightful reading for young and old.

Their source is the subject of some controversy in Brazil. Couto de Magalhães, an authority on the Amazon and its people, classified them as Indian tales. Sylvio Romero, a Brazilian collector of folklore, also so considered them, as did the great explorer of the region, Charles Frederick Hartt.

Hartt is of the opinion that these tales represent solar myths brought to Brazil from Asia—that Jabotí personifies the sun, and the deer, Suasú, represents the moon. More recent writers, like Nina Rodriguez and Arthur Ramos, attribute these tales to African slaves brought to Brazil by the Portuguese.

Whatever the true source, the fact remains that these legends were known to different tribes of Indians from the Amazon to the Paraguay rivers. Both de Magalhães and Hartt gathered similar tales in the nineteenth century from Indians—who had little or no contact with whites or blacks—in places remote from areas of civilization such as the Paraguay River, the Rio Negro, and the Tapajós River, all of which tends to disprove the African origin.

Whatever the origin, this series in which Jabotí, the tortoise, plays the principal role, is a valuable contribution to the folklore of the Americas.

Lena F. Hurlong

Jabotí, the Tortoise, Wins a Race

1 In the Amazon jungle there was a tortoise and his name was Jabotí. He sat at the base of a palm tree playing his flute and he was happy.

Jabotí and his flute were always together. He played it in the dry season and he played it in the rainy season. All the other animals envied him and would have done anything to have the instrument. But though Jabotí was a kind fellow and would do anything for anybody, he wouldn't give up his flute. Oh, no, not his flute!

The flute was to Jabotí what gold is to a miser, what a song is to a bird. If anyone tried to take it from him . . . and many did . . . he would fight like mad. Once the jaguar did take it . . . but that's another story.

On this particular day, Jabotí was on his way to visit his cousin. He played his flute as he went. In a clearing he met Suasú, the deer.

"Hello, Jabotí," greeted the fleet-footed animal. "Where are you going on this bright day?"

"Oh, good morning," answered Jabotí politely. "I'm on my way to visit my cousin who lives at the other side of this clearing. I haven't seen him for a long time."

"Where did you get that flute?" went on the deer.

"I made it from the bone of a jaguar I killed."

Jabotí spoke as if killing a jaguar was as easy as playing the flute.

"You killed a jaguar! Do you expect me to believe you killed a jaguar?"

"Yes, I did."

"Why, you couldn't kill a fly. Everyone knows you're no match for any animal in the jungle."

"Is that so?" snapped the quick-tempered tortoise. "You may think I'm weak, but you're wrong." Then he thought a while. "Suppose you tell me what it is *you* can do best of all," he asked at last.

"I can run," said Suasú puzzled by the question.

"All right. Then we'll run a race."

Suasú laughed out loud. "Ha, ha, ha! Ho, ho, ho! Ha, ha, ha!"

"You laugh, but I dare you . . . I repeat . . . I dare you to run a race with me."

"Do you really mean it? You're not joking, are you?" asked the deer.

"Of course I mean it."

"Very well, let's begin. You run here and I'll . . . ."

"Oh, no, not now," interrupted Jabotí quickly. "I have too many things to do today. We'll race tomorrow. Besides, I'll show you how fair I can be. You can't run in the forest because there are too many vines. So you'll run in this clearing and I'll run in the forest not far from the edge. When you want to know where I am, all you need do is call out and I'll answer you. What do you say to that?" finished the cunning tortoise.

"Why, that's more than fair. I'm satisfied. You run in the woods and I'll run in the clearing. But I'll enter the race on one condition and on one condition only."

"What condition?" asked Jabotí suspiciously.

"The winner is to get the flute."

Jabotí hesitated. His flute, his beloved flute . . . what if he should lose his flute! But he had gone too far. He couldn't draw back now.

"Agreed," he said bravely, though he had a funny feeling in the region of his heart.

That night, Jabotí called all of his aunts and uncles, his first and second cousins, his parents and grandparents, his friends and every tortoise he could reach. They came together in front of his cousin's house. Some sat on rocks, others on fallen trunks of trees. The greatest number settled themselves comfortably among the leaves. All were eager to hear what Jabotí had to say.

Jabotí spoke very seriously. "Friends and relatives," he began, "this is a very serious meeting. The reputation of our family is at stake . . . nay, more, the reputation of every tortoise in the Amazon jungle, to say nothing of the reputation of those who live in other parts of the world."

His words were greeted by a rustling of leaves and excited whispers. Jabotí could feel how nervous they all were as they waited for him to continue.

"Tomorrow . . ." Jabotí paused to let his words sink in, "tomorrow, I run a race with Suasú, the deer."

"Stupid!" "Foolish!" "Insane!" came from every side. One old tortoise, not able to stand it any longer, asked for permission to speak. Everyone was silent.

"My friends," he said sadly, "my friends, it is clear to me that Jabotí has gone mad—that he has lost his senses. He has dared to challenge the deer to run a race with him. That proves he is insane. I suggest that we call together a council of the older members to decide what shall be done with him. Unless we do something, he will surely get us into more serious trouble."

Before anyone could answer, Jabotí spoke up quickly. "Just a minute, everybody. I don't blame you for feeling as you do. But first let me finish what I have to say."

The others agreed it was only fair that Jabotí be allowed to defend himself.

In a whisper he told them his plan. They all listened eagerly.

The next day was bright and sunny. Suasú came early although she was sure Jabotí wouldn't turn up. All of a sudden she thought she heard Jabotí's voice come from the jungle.

"Good morning, friend Suasú. Here I am all ready to go. I'll do the counting. Ready?"

"Ready," echoed the surprised deer.

"One . . . two . . . three . . . go!"

Suasú was so sure she would win the race easily that she began to walk along the racecourse very slowly. She had walked only a little way when she looked back and called, "Jabotí." Imagine her surprise when a voice came to her from the jungle —ahead of her! "Here I am . . . ahead of you. You'd better hurry if you want to keep up with me."

"What do you think of that?" the deer said to herself. "How did he get so far ahead of me?" She ran a bit faster.

After a time she called again. Again a voice answered, "Here I am, Suasú."

Suasú began to worry. She ran faster and faster, as if the jaguar were chasing her. "Surely this time I've passed him," she muttered to herself. But when she called again, again she heard a voice that came from the jungle some distance in front of her, "Here I am, Suasú."

And so the race continued . . . the deer running with all her might . . . the deer calling. A tortoise answering . . . the answer coming always from the jungle ahead of her . . . always, always ahead of her . . . until Suasú could go no farther. She lay down, completely worn-out, not far from the end of the racecourse.

There Jabotí found her with her tongue hanging out, gasping for breath.

"Well," said Jabotí, "who would have believed that I, a tortoise, could win a race against you, a deer! You thought you could get my flute, did you? Look at you, so worn-out you can't move, while I feel fresh enough to start another race right now. What's more, I dare you to run another race with me this minute."

"Oh, no, for pity's sake," begged Suasú. "Go! Leave me! I can't go another step. Keep your flute. I don't want it anyway."

Jabotí was delighted. His plan had worked even better than he had expected. Not one of his relatives had failed him. His aunts, his uncles, his first cousins, his second cousins, his parents, his grandparents and his friends had followed his instructions to the letter. Each had taken his place along the route, keeping about fifty feet apart. Each time Suasú called Jabotí, the tortoise ahead of the deer answered.

Jabotí took his flute from his pocket, put it to his lips, and away he went playing a merry tune for all the world to hear.

The Alligator Likes Honey

2 It was the rainy season on the Amazon. It rained by day. It rained by night. It rained so much that the waters of the river overflowed their banks and reached far, far into the jungle. It rained so hard that great chunks of land broke off from the sides of the river and went floating out to sea.

It rained and rained but Jabotí was happy. He liked to stick his feet in the soft earth and wiggle his toes about. He liked to smell the freshness of the clean, fragrant air. He liked to eat the fruit that ripened during the rainy season. He liked the rainy season so much that he composed new music for his flute, and went through the forest playing it.

When the vulture heard him, he said, "Lucky Jabotí! How I wish I had your flute!"

When the monkey heard him, he exclaimed, "I wish I had a flute like that."

When the jaguar heard him, he roared, "I'd give anything to have Jabotí's flute."

But Jabotí only laughed and played louder.

When he reached the water's edge, Jacaré, the alligator, heard him. He muttered to himself, "I'll find a way to get that flute from Jabotí." To Jabotí, he said, "Hello, Jabotí. You seem happy this morning."

"Good morning," said Jabotí politely. "Yes, I am very happy. That's why I'm playing my flute."

"Come closer," said the thick-skinned monster. "Come closer so that I can hear you better."

Jabotí went closer to Jacaré and played another piece on his flute. He played something like this, "La, la, la. Mi, mi, mi."

"My, how beautifully you play," said Jacaré enviously. "You are clever, Jabotí. It's a pity you're so selfish."

"Selfish? What do you mean, Jacaré?" snapped Jabotí. "I'm not selfish."

"Oh, yes, you are," repeated the alligator. "You can't deny it. You are selfish."

Jabotí was hurt. "In what way am I selfish? Tell me, in what way am I selfish?"

"If I asked you to do me a small kindness you would refuse," said Jacaré.

"Try me, only try me."

"All right, I'll try you. But it won't do any good because I know how selfish you are."

"Don't say that again," commanded Jabotí who really was an obliging fellow. "Just tell me what you want me to do for you."

"I warn you, you'll say no."

"Oh, don't talk so much. Tell me what you want."

"I want you to lend me your flute."

"My flute," gasped Jabotí in surprise. "My flute! You want me to lend you my flute?"

"Just long enough to play one tune on it . . . only one short tune. But I knew it would be no use asking you . . . you're so selfish."

Poor Jabotí was troubled. He didn't want to lend the flute to anybody, especially not to the alligator, but he certainly didn't want anybody to think he was selfish. "Now listen to me, Jacaré. I love my flute. But I'm not selfish." He paused, then continued, "I'll lend it to you, if you promise to give it back to me as soon as you play one piece on it."

"Yes, I'll give it back to you right away," promised Jacaré, though the wicked creature had no intention of giving back the flute at all.

No sooner did the alligator put his hand on the flute than . . . splash . . . he was in the water.

The flute was gone.

Poor Jabotí! He was heartbroken when he realized what Jacaré had done. He wanted to cry. What should he do now? How could he get his flute back? This was what came of being generous with a creature as wicked as Jacaré.

The tortoise paced the riverbank, back and forth, back and forth. Suddenly on a branch nearby, he noticed a beehive. One of the bees called out, "What's the matter, Jabotí? Why are you so unhappy?"

"Good morning, Mr. Bee," said Jabotí. "That mean Jacaré ran away with my flute."

"Why did you give it to him? You know you can't trust him."

"He said I was selfish if I didn't lend it to him."

"You, selfish! Why, my good friend, Jabotí, everyone knows how good and kind you are. What are you going to do about the flute now?"

"I don't know. I don't know," repeated the unhappy Jabotí over and over again.

Jabotí thought and thought and thought. At last

he decided to take a desperate chance. "I think, friend bee," he said, "I think I can get my flute back if you will help me."

"I'll do anything I can, friend Jabotí," answered the bee.

"Thank you," said Jabotí. "All I want is a little bit of your honey," went on the tortoise.

"Is that all?" said the bee. "Help yourself to all I have."

Jabotí took some honey from the bee, put it on the ground and stuck his tail in it. He turned and turned his tail about until it had a thick layer of honey on it. Then he went back to where the alligator had been. Jabotí dug a hole and buried himself in it, that is, all but his tail. His tail stuck out like a stick of honey. With his hands he grasped a root. Jabotí had taken some bees with him, too, so they could fly about and buzz when Jacaré came to the surface. Jacaré would think it was a real honeycomb. "You begin buzzing when I tell you to," explained Jabotí to the bees.

"All right," they agreed. "We'll gladly help you trick that bad alligator."

After a while, Jacaré cautiously stuck his head out of the water. He didn't see the tortoise. "He's gone," he said to himself. "I can come out now. Anyway, the flute is safe in my house at the bottom of the river. He can't get it no matter how hard he tries."

Clumsily, he made his way to the bank to take his daily nap. As he was about to fall asleep with his mouth wide open, an aroma reached his nostrils. He sniffed the air. "What is that?" he asked himself. "It smells like honey."

At that moment Jabotí told the bees to fly about and buzz. Jacaré heard them.

"It is honey. Just listen to the bees. But where is it?"

He searched here and he searched there. Finally, he saw a pile of honey within easy reach. Of course

he didn't know the honey was on Jabotí's tail. He thought it was a bit of honey that had fallen from a beehive somewhere high up on a tree.

The tortoise lay very quiet waiting for the alligator to come for the honey. As soon as Jabotí felt Jacaré's hand on his tail, he pressed his two shells together catching Jacaré's finger between them.

"Ouch," yelled Jacaré. "Let go my finger. Let go, whoever you are."

"I am Jabotí. I won't let go your finger until you return my flute."

"Let go, I tell you," screamed the alligator. "I haven't got your flute. It's in the water."

"I don't care where it is. I want my flute, and I won't let go until you give it to me," said Jabotí, and he squeezed harder.

"I'll get even with you for this," said Jacaré angrily. He pulled with all his might, but Jabotí clung to the root and squeezed tighter.

"If you try pulling me out of this hole, I'll break your finger," warned Jabotí.

Jacaré tried and tried but it was no use. Every time he pulled, Jabotí squeezed harder until the alligator thought his finger would break. Finally, he couldn't stand the pain any longer. He called to his eldest son, Gonçalo. "Oh, Gonçalo," he screamed, "bring me the flute."

Gonçalo didn't understand what his father said. "What is it you want?" he asked from across the river where he was resting under a giant lily pad. "Do you want your coat?"

"No, no, no. The flute, Jabotí's flute," shouted Jacaré.

"Do you want your trousers?" asked Gonçalo.

"No, no. Please hurry. Bring Jabotí's flute."

"Oh," said Gonçalo. "You want your boots. Why didn't you say so the first time?"

"No, no, no . . . ouch . . ." screamed the unhappy alligator louder than ever. "It's the flute I want."

At last, the lazy Gonçalo came close enough to hear what his father really wanted. "Oh, the flute. All right. Wait a minute and I'll get it for you."

In a little while, he came up with the flute.

"Bring it here," said Jacaré hoping his son would help him capture Jabotí.

Jabotí was frightened. He knew what the alligator intended to do. "Don't you dare tell him I'm here," warned Jabotí. "Ask him to throw the flute to you or I'll break off your finger."

"All right. All right. Don't squeeze anymore."

27

Then he called to Gonçalo. "Don't bring the flute here. Just throw it."

This pleased the lazy Gonçalo who was anxious to get back to his lily pad. So he threw the flute to his father and hurried back into the water.

Jacaré picked up the flute with his free hand and placed it where Jabotí could reach it.

As soon as the tortoise had the flute, he let go of Jacaré's finger and dug deep, deep into the hole where the alligator couldn't reach him.

Jacaré's finger was sore. It was so sore it made him walk on three legs. He groaned and moaned. "My finger. My finger. My poor, poor finger. You'll be sorry for this, Jabotí."

"Oh, your finger will be all right as soon as you get into the water."

Jacaré threw the tortoise an angry look and, disgusted with himself, went into the river.

Jabotí went to the water's edge, took a drink, then, happy as a bird, turned and went playing his flute through the jungle.

Jabotí on the Treetop

3 It was daybreak on the Amazon. The birds sang. The insects hummed. The alligators stood guard over their eggs. Even the lazy boa constrictors raised their heads to look at the rising sun. All nature was stirring, for the sun, like a huge Chinese lantern, would soon appear above the treetops.

Jabotí, the tortoise, was hurrying through the forest, playing the flute as he went. He was on his way to the inajá palm tree to eat some fruit. For Jabotí liked fruit. He liked all kinds of fruit. He liked bananas. He liked melons. He liked pineapples. But best of all he liked the fruit of the inajá palm. That's why he was going so fast. He was afraid the tapir might get there before him and eat the ripened fruit that had fallen to the ground during the night.

"It's a good thing," he said to himself as he ran.

"It's a good thing that ripe fruit falls to the ground. If it didn't, I'd never have a chance to eat any."

As soon as he reached the inajá palm tree, he began a careful search. He searched here. He searched there. But not one fruit could he find.

The more he searched, the hungrier he became. The more he looked at the great bunches of fruit hanging from the tree, the more his mouth watered.

"How I wish I could climb like a monkey," he said to himself. "I'd scurry up that tree like lightning and eat and eat and eat. I'd jump from one bunch to another as easily as a bird flies. I'd choose only the best and ripest fruit and throw the rest to the ground. Oh, how I wish I were a monkey!"

The more he thought about it, the more he felt he had been badly treated by the great god Tupana when the earth and the animals were made.

He looked hungrily at the fruit for a long time. At last he said to himself in disgust, "I might just as well go home. There's no use staying here any longer."

Just as he turned to go, he heard a sound. He looked up. Sure enough, there on the inajá palm sat a monkey. He was eating the juicy fruit to his heart's content. Jabotí couldn't help being jealous but he said politely, "Good morning, Mr. Macaco. How is the fruit this morning?"

"Delicious!" answered the monkey smacking his lips together.

"Won't you please throw some fruit down for me?" begged Jabotí eagerly.

"Why don't you come up and get some for yourself?" laughed the monkey, knowing very well Jabotí couldn't climb trees.

"Oh, I could climb the tree if I wanted to," snapped Jabotí quickly. "It's just that I'm not feeling very well today. Please, Mr. Macaco," he coaxed, "please throw some fruit down for me."

"I'll do better than that," said the mischievous monkey. "I'll come down and carry you up here; then you can eat all you want."

"All right," said Jabotí.

No sooner said than done. With a few jumps, and a few swings by the tail, the monkey came down, grabbed Jabotí gingerly by one leg and carried him up to the top of the inajá palm tree—almost a hundred feet from the ground. Then he set him down on a big bunch of fruit and went away.

Jabotí's heart began to beat fast, but he was happy. His wish had come true. At last, he could eat all the fruit he wanted. He could pick and choose as he pleased. So he ate and ate until he couldn't eat anymore. Then he called, "Friend Macaco, I'm ready to go down now. Come and get me!"

He listened for an answer. No answer came. He called again, "Macaco, Macaco," but no Macaco did he see. Frightened, he looked everywhere. The monkey was gone!

Poor Jabotí was terribly frightened. How was he ever to get down from the inajá palm tree? He could see himself sitting on that tree year after year . . . this year . . . next . . . the year after that, . . . but he couldn't think any further ahead.

Jabotí clung to that bunch of inajá fruit all that day. He clung to it all that night. He clung to it all the next morning. He clung to it so long his feet and hands were numb.

"I just can't hold on any longer. I'm getting dizzy," he said to himself at last. "I'll just have to shut my eyes and let go, no matter what happens."

He got ready to jump when he heard footsteps. He opened his eyes and looked down. There under the tree stood Yareté, the jaguar.

Jabotí had never been so glad to see anyone before. "The great god Tupana must have sent him here just to help me," he said happily. "Let me think. Let me think. I must find a way to use the jaguar to help me get down from here, but how?"

Yareté, the jaguar, had seen Jabotí on the palm tree. He called, "Hello, Jabotí. How did you get way up there?"

"I climbed up, of course. How do you think I got up here? This fruit is delicious. I have had a wonderful dinner. Now I'm ready to come down."

"Don't come down yet," begged the jaguar. "Throw me down some fruit first."

Then and there Jabotí decided what he was going to do.

"All right, Yareté," said Jabotí. "I'll throw some fruit down to you, but you must come closer. Stand right there, under me so you can catch the fruit and keep it from hitting the ground."

"All right, Jabotí. Where do you want me to stand . . . here?"

"No, just a little closer to the trunk of the tree . . . there . . . that's it, right there."

When the jaguar had placed himself directly under Jabotí, the tortoise called out, "Stay there, now! Don't move! Get ready to catch the fruit. Here goes: One . . . two . . . three."

Instead of throwing fruit, the cunning tortoise threw himself down, smack down on Yareté, the jaguar.

The jaguar was stunned. He was so stunned, he couldn't grab Jabotí though the tortoise was right there in front of him. Before the jaguar knew what had happened, Jabotí was running for dear life in the direction of his hole, thanking the great god Tupana for having saved his life.

Finally Yareté pulled himself together and started

to run after Jabotí. He reached the hole just as Jabotí slipped into it. Quickly, Yareté stuck his hand into the hole and grabbed something! It was Jaboti's leg!

Jabotí was frightened. He was so frightened, his knees shook, but he put on a brave front. "Well, Yareté," he said as calmly as he could. "You think you're clever, don't you? You think you're holding on to my leg. Ha, ha, ha! The joke is on you. It isn't my leg at all . . . it's a root."

The stupid jaguar believed what Jabotí told him. He let go of his leg. Quick as a flash, Jabotí went deeper, deeper into the hole, so deep the jaguar couldn't reach him.

Yareté was furious. "You tricked me again," he said showing his teeth. "But you can't win all the time. I won't leave here until you come out. I'll stay here until doomsday. You'll have to come out sometime. And when you do, I'll get even with you. See if I don't."

The jaguar forgot one thing. He forgot that a tortoise can go without food much longer than a jaguar can. Yareté waited and waited until his stomach growled for food. At last, he was so hungry he couldn't stand it any longer. He looked about him for help. In a tree close by, he saw a vulture. His name was Urubú.

Yareté called to him. "Good morning, Urubú. Will you do something for me?"

"Yes, if you'll tell me what it is," answered the grouchy vulture.

"Urubú, will you please come down here and keep an eye on this opening?" he asked. "Jabotí is in there. If he tries to leave the hole, call me. I won't be far away and I'll come at once."

When the vulture came down and stood by the opening of the hole, Yareté went off for his dinner.

Jabotí waited long enough for the jaguar to get out of sight, then he stuck his nose slowly out of the hole. Two big, ugly eyes met his. He shivered, but he knew this was his only chance to get away. He just had to do something before the jaguar returned.

Quickly, he gathered some dirt into a pile. Then he came as near the opening of the hole as he dared. "Oh, Urubú," he coaxed, "please come closer. I have something good for you. You'll like it, I know."

"Just be sure you don't try any of your tricks on me," said the vulture.

"Oh, I wouldn't think of playing a trick on such a clever bird as you are," said the cunning tortoise. "It's just that I have something for you, something you like."

The greedy vulture, not knowing what Jabotí was about to do, went closer to the hole. At once Jabotí took up a handful of dirt and threw it with all his might at the surprised vulture.

Urubú put his hands over his eyes and cried, "I can't see! I can't see!"

Jabotí came out of his hole as fast as he could.

The vulture rubbed and rubbed his eyes.

Jabotí slipped quietly into the thick underbrush.

Urubú called excitedly, "Yareté, Yareté, come quickly!"

Yareté came running as fast as he could. "What's the matter, Urubú? Why are you yelling so?"

The vulture didn't say a word. He just pointed to the empty hole.

Yareté saw at once that the tortoise was gone. "What's happened to Jabotí?" he asked sternly.

"He threw dirt at me and ran away," explained the disgusted vulture.

Yareté was angry. He was so angry, he let out a roar that frightened the birds. But it was no use. Jabotí had escaped. The jaguar hunted and hunted but he knew that it wouldn't do any good. Trying to find Jabotí in the Amazon jungle was like trying to find a needle in a haystack.

Meanwhile, Jabotí had reached a safe place. He took out his flute, and was dancing a special jig all by himself.

Jabotí
Takes a Wife

4 Jabotí, the tortoise, was sad. He didn't know why he was sad but he was. He was so sad, he sat for hours on the banks of the Amazon playing sad music on his flute. All the fishes came up to the surface to hear him.

"Very good music," said the deep voice of the alligator.

"Lovely," piped the shrill voice of the tiger fish.

"Lovely but sad," said the river porpoise who knew a great deal about such things.

When Jabotí finished playing, he put his head on his foot and gave a deep sigh.

The river porpoise asked, "What's the matter, Jabotí? Are you lonesome?"

"Yes, I am, my good friend," answered the tortoise.

"If you're lonesome, why don't you marry? Everyone should marry," said the river porpoise.

The other fishes nodded their heads in approval. "Yes, of course, everyone should marry," they echoed.

Jabotí looked up in surprise. It was such a new idea. He turned the idea over and over in his mind. At last he said, "Yes, I will. I'll get married." Then he paused, "But whom shall I marry?"

"Why not marry the daughter of the jaguar?" said the alligator, who liked a big, strong wife.

"Oh, no," said Jabotí, "'her father may come home someday in a temper and just scoop me out

of my shell with one stroke of his paw. That would be the end of poor Jabotí. No, no, not the daughter of the jaguar."

"Well then, why not marry the daughter of the monkey?" suggested the tiger fish.

"No, that won't do either. She would chatter all the time. I shouldn't have a moment's peace."

"Why not the daughter of the anteater?"

"And have my food and the whole house full of ants? No, thank you."

"The daughter of the cutia?"

"No, she would always be playing some trick on me. She is very mischievous . . . let me see . . . let me see. Whom shall I marry?"

He thought and thought and thought. At last he jumped up as if a bee had stung him. "I know. I know. I shall marry Suasú, the daughter of the deer. She is gentle. She is kind. She will make a good wife."

Before his river friends could say anything, Jabotí had waved good-bye and was on his way.

He went directly to the house of Suasú. The door was opened by Suasú's mother, Mrs. Deer.

"May I come in?" asked Jabotí politely.

"Yes, of course you may. You are always welcome, friend Jabotí. Come in."

Jabotí went in and sat down. He moved his feet this way and that way. He hemmed. He hawed. He coughed. He tried very hard but he couldn't get up the courage to say a thing.

Mrs. Deer could see he had something special to tell her, so she helped him. "Is there anything you want to say to me, Jabotí?" she asked kindly.

"Yes, there is, Mrs. Deer," stammered Jabotí. Then he went on very fast, "I want to marry your daughter, Suasú."

"Dear, dear," said Suasú's mother gently. "You are a day too late. Only yesterday, Suasú became engaged to Yareté, the jaguar. You know our daughter is very charming, the most charming, we might say, in the entire Amazon region."

"Yes, yes. She is charming, I know," agreed Jabotí.

"We felt that only the best, the strongest and the wisest creature should become her husband. And you must admit there is none wiser, nor stronger, nor more handsome than Yareté, the jaguar."

Jabotí said politely but firmly, "I don't agree with

you. Yareté, the jaguar, is not as strong nor as wise as he pretends to be."

"You must be mistaken, Jabotí," said Mrs. Deer. "How can that be? Everyone is afraid of him."

"Well, *I'm* not. And what's more, he does whatever I ask him to do. When I speak, he jumps up to obey. I can ride him about as if he were a donkey."

"Is that true, Jabotí?" gasped Mrs. Deer in surprise.

"Indeed it is, Mrs. Deer. What's more, I'll prove it to you." Then he asked, "But if I prove this to you, may I marry your daughter, Suasú?"

"Oh, yes," said Suasú's mother. "If you can prove that you are stronger and braver than Yareté, the jaguar, you may marry Suasú."

Jabotí said, "Thank you," very politely and went off into the jungle. Then his troubles began. It was all very well to boast of riding the king of the jungle—for in his heart Jabotí knew the jaguar was the king of the jungle—but how was he to do it? How? That was the question.

He rested his head on one foot and thought and thought and thought. No plan came to him. He rested his head on the other foot . . . still no idea came to him. Then, he raised his head to the sun and . . . snap. . . . just like that . . . he knew what he was to do.

Mrs. Deer had told him that she was expecting a visit from Yareté that same afternoon. Jabotí knew the path the jaguar would take. He tied a handkerchief about his head and lay directly in the path. When he saw Yareté coming, he began to moan.

"What's the matter, Jabotí?" asked Yareté.

"Oh . . . Oh . . ." moaned the tortoise, "I don't feel very well."

"Too bad," said Yareté. "I am on my way to see Suasú. Would you like to go with me?"

"I'd like to go with you very much, but I can't walk that far. I feel sick, but . . ." he continued quickly, "if you'll carry me, I'll go."

"I'll carry you part of the way," said the jaguar.

"Stoop down then and let me climb up your back," said Jabotí, laughing inside.

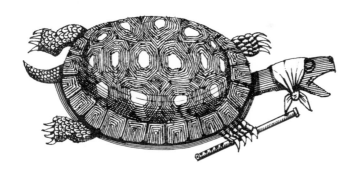

The jaguar stooped and Jabotí climbed up onto his back. After they had gone a few steps, Jabotí fell to the ground.

"What's the matter, Jabotí? Can't you stay on my back?"

"No, I'm too weak. Why don't you tie a vine around your waist? Then I can hold on to that."

"Very well, I'll tie a vine around my waist," said the jaguar. So he found a vine and tied it about his body.

Jabotí again climbed up the jaguar's back and hung on to the vine. After a while he said, "Yareté, why don't you get me a switch? A rider should have a switch, shouldn't he?"

The jaguar chuckled. He was in very good spirits today. "You are a funny little fellow, Jabotí. All right, I'll do what you say." He cut a switch and gave it to the tortoise.

Jabotí rode the jaguar quietly until they came before the house of Suasú.

Yareté said, "Jabotí, you can get off now and walk the rest of the way."

Instead of getting off, Jabotí threw the bandage from his head and stood straight up on Yareté's back. He grasped the switch and struck it smartly

against the sides of the jaguar. He struck him on one side. He struck him on the other side, all the time shouting "Giddap! Giddap!"

The jaguar became angry. "What's the matter with you, Jabotí? Are you going mad?"

Jabotí yelled louder than ever. He wanted to be sure Suasú's mother heard him. "Never mind answering back, Yareté. You do as I say . . . just keep moving."

By this time, Yareté knew he had been tricked. He was very, very angry. And when he saw that Mr. and Mrs. Deer and Suasú herself were standing in front of their house watching everything that was going on, he was angrier than ever. He would have liked to take Jabotí by the neck and scoop him out of his shell once and for all. He tried and tried but he couldn't reach Jabotí who was hanging on for dear life to the vine that the jaguar had tied around his own body. At last Yareté gave up trying to reach Jabotí. Jumping and kicking, he galloped off into the jungle, trying all the time to shake off the mischievous tortoise from his back.

Jabotí clung to the vine until he saw one of his many holes in the ground. Then he slipped down silently. Down into the hole he went, before the jaguar could grab him.

Yareté saw where Jabotí went but he was too late. Jabotí had gone so deep into the hole, the jaguar couldn't reach him. So Yareté, with his tail between his legs, slunk off into the jungle, disgusted with himself and disgusted with the world, muttering bitterly, "I'll get you someday, Jabotí. I'll get you."

When Jabotí saw that the jaguar had gone, he came out of the hole and hurried to the house of Mr. and Mrs. Deer. When he reached there, he said proudly, "What did I tell you? I am braver and stronger than the jaguar, Mrs. Deer. You saw with your own eyes how I rode Yareté as if he were a donkey. Now may I marry Suasú?"

"If Suasú is willing," said Mrs. Deer slowly.

"Yes, Suasú must be willing," said Mr. Deer.

Suasú was willing. So they were married at once. Afterwards they went to live in a section of the forest where the jaguar could never find them.

Jabotí played his flute. Suasú did the cooking. Jabotí's music was no longer sad. It was cheerful and gay for Jabotí wasn't lonely anymore.

The Tug of War

5   Jabotí, the tortoise, was wise. He was the wisest creature in the whole world . . . well, anyway, in the Amazon jungle. He was so wise no matter how hard the other animals tried they could never get the better of him.

One bright, sunshiny day Jabotí started for the river. On the way he stopped long enough to say hello to an ant, to help a bird pull a stubborn worm from the ground, to settle a quarrel between two monkeys, and even found time to gossip with the butterflies.

He had been so busy talking, he didn't notice a tamerebá tree until he was almost under it. "My!" he muttered as he quickly changed his course. "I almost passed right under that tree."

A monkey chattering in the branches saw him and called, "Hi, there, Jabotí. Why are you running away? Afraid of me?"

"Afraid of you? I am Jabotí, the tortoise. I'm afraid of nobody. It's this tree I'm avoiding."

"You must be losing your senses. A tree can't hurt you."

"Oh, can't it? This tree can. What if it were to fall on me and pin me down?"

"What difference would that make to you? All you have to do is wait for it to decay and then get up and walk away as if nothing had happened. You've done it before."

"Yes, that's true about the other trees but not this one. This is the taperebá. When this one falls, it sends out shoots that take root in the ground. If this one were to pin me down, I'd stay pinned down until I was dead as a stone. That happened to one of my cousins and I ought to know. No, thank you. I'll keep away from this tree."

At the river's edge, he began to drink deeply. Nearby, an enormous alligator was swimming about swishing his tail this way and that . . . just having a gay, merry time. When he saw the tortoise, he called out, "Hi, there, you undersized worm, what are you doing near the water?"

Jabotí lost his temper easily. "What do you think I'm doing?" he snapped. "I'm thirsty and I've come down to drink. Is there anything strange about that, Mr. Jacaré? Moreover, I'll ask you not to call me an 'undersized worm'—I don't like it."

Jacaré began to laugh.

"Why are you laughing, you big bully?" demanded Jabotí as sternly as he could.

"I'm laughing at you. What can you do about it?" retorted the thick-skinned monster. "Look at those stumpy legs and that crazy-quilt body. What good are you to the world?"

Jabotí was hurt. "You think you're smart just because you're twelve feet long and weigh a ton. Well, that doesn't mean *that* to me," and he snapped his fingers to prove how little it did mean.

Rage filled Jabotí's heart. He became reckless.

"I'm stronger than you are, Jacaré, short legs or no short legs."

"Stronger than I am! Listen to that. That's good. Ha, ha, ha. Oh, I shall die laughing."

"Laugh if you want to. Just the same I know I can pull you out of the water as easily as I can shake my tail."

Jacaré laughed out loud. "Look who's boasting. Why, with one swish of my tail I can send you spinning to the other end of the world. Pull *me* out of the water! You don't know what you're saying."

Jacaré decided to test Jabotí's strength. "Very well, let's see you do it."

"Not so fast, my friend. Just wait until I go back into the forest and get a stout vine. Then you'll pull one end and I'll pull at the other and we'll see . . . what we shall see."

Jabotí hurried away into the jungle out of sight of the alligator. He ran as fast as his funny little legs could carry him. He was deeply troubled. "Jabotí," he said to himself sternly. "I always suspected you were foolish. Now I know you are. Challenge an alligator! You haven't the sense you were born with. Now do something and do it quickly."

He thought hard. No idea came to him. He thought some more. Still no idea. He tried again. Then a plan came to him. "I have it," he said aloud. "But I shall need the help of the tapir. Fortunately, I know where to find him."

Tapira, the tapir, saw the tortoise coming. Jabotí was all out of breath.

"Why are you hurrying?" Tapira asked curiously. "Is something chasing you?"

"Nothing is chasing me. I am Jabotí, the tortoise,

and everyone is afraid of me," said Jabotí proudly. "I'm looking for you."

"For me? What do you want with me?"

"You know Jacaré, the huge alligator that swims down near our drinking hole? Well, I don't like to tell tales . . . but he's been telling everyone that he's stronger than you are. He says he can easily pull you into the river."

"Why, that . . . that . . . boaster." Tapira was angry. "With one tug, I'd have him out on dry land and begging for mercy. Pull me into the water, indeed!"

"That's what I said but he laughed at me. And he's telling all the animals that you're a coward and are afraid of him."

"Is that so? I'll show him. Where is he? Take me where he is."

"Wait, wait," begged the now thoroughly frightened tortoise. "Don't go down there! I'll take care of everything. You wait here while I cut down a strong vine. Then you take one end and Jacaré will take the other and we'll see who can pull harder."

"Oh, all right, if you think it best," answered the tapir. "But I want you to understand this. I'm not afraid of that clumsy boaster anywhere, not on land nor in the water."

"I know, I know, but you do as I say and we'll cure that troublemaker of his conceit."

Jabotí then went stumbling along through the woods to return presently with a very long, thick vine. He tied one end securely around the body of the tapir.

"Now," he ordered. "Wait here until I go down

and tie the other end to the tail of the alligator. When you feel a tug, you pull with all your might."

Jabotí was beginning to enjoy himself very much.

Having tied Tapira, he took the other end and fastened it to the tail of Jacaré, the alligator. When that was done, he said, "Now you wait until I go back into the jungle where the other end is. I'll shake the vine. That will be the signal for you to pull. And you'd better pull hard because I'm going to drag you to the shore."

At a place midway between Tapira and Jacaré,

Jabotí shook the vine. Then he hid behind a bush to see what would happen.

Jacaré and Tapira began to pull.

What a tug of war that was! Jacaré swam with all his might to the middle of the river. He dragged the tapir almost to the edge of the forest. Then the tapir got a foothold and drew Jacaré toward the shore.

Jacaré pulled and Tapira pulled. Jacaré pulled again, and Tapira pulled again while Jabotí laughed until he cried. They kept on, tugging one against the other, for what seemed like ages and ages. At last, they were completely worn out. Tapira lay on his back panting. Jacaré could scarcely move his tail.

At that very moment, Jabotí came out of hiding. Quickly he untied the tapir, saying kindly, "Do you feel all right?"

"I feel terrible. I had no idea Jacaré was so strong." Then he asked anxiously, "It was a draw, wasn't it? We were even, weren't we? Jacaré didn't pull me into the water, did he?"

"No, he didn't. However, you had better go home now and get some rest. I'll see what's happened to Jacaré."

Terribly disappointed, Tapira disappeared into the jungle.

Jabotí found Jacaré on the shore with his mouth wide open. He was breathing hard. When he saw the tortoise looking as fresh as if he had just had a nap, he exclaimed in surprise, "Why, you don't look tired at all. I just can't believe it. How can a little fellow like you be so powerful?"

"Well, Mr. Jacaré, what do you think now? Will you admit I'm stronger than you are?"

"Yes, yes, I admit it," said the alligator, but he was puzzled just the same.

Jabotí untied the vine from the alligator's tail. He went off very well pleased with himself, leaving poor Jacaré muttering, "It can't be true. It just can't be true."

Meanwhile Jabotí walked proudly through the jungle in search of his friends, the butterflies, and was soon busily gossiping with them, as if nothing had happened.

The Magic Tree

6 Jabotí, the tortoise, was curious. He was the most curious creature in the Amazon jungle. He was so curious he wanted to know everything, even the secret of the magic tree.

The magic tree stood on the banks of the Amazon River. On it was the most delicious fruit in the world. But this tree was different from other trees. It had a magic all its own. No matter how hard Jabotí tried, he couldn't get any fruit from the magic tree.

One morning, bright and early, he set out. "I won't come back until I learn the secret of that tree," he said to himself as he plodded his way through the jungle. He remembered to take his flute with him, for Jabotí never went anywhere without his flute.

Under a coconut palm, he met Macaco, the monkey.

"Where are you going so early, friend Jabotí?" asked the monkey.

"I'm going to the magic tree for some fruit," explained the tortoise.

"Do you know the name of the magic tree?" asked Macaco.

"No, I don't—but what difference does that make?"

"It makes a great deal of difference. Don't you know that you can't pick fruit from the magic tree unless you can pronounce its name clearly out loud?" asked the monkey in surprise.

"No, I didn't know that, friend Macaco."

"Well, its true. Just the other day I tried to pluck a fruit but the more I pulled, the harder the fruit stuck to the tree."

"Since that is so," said Jabotí, "will you please tell me the name of the magic tree?"

"The name? I wish I knew it," sighed the monkey.

"Don't you know it?" asked Jabotí disappointed.

"No, I don't, but I know who does know it."

"Who?" asked Jabotí. "Tell me who knows it!"

"Curica, the green parrot, is the only one who knows the name of the magic tree. She lives on the banks of the river not far from the tree itself."

"I'll go to her at once and ask for the name," said Jabotí.

"Not so fast, my friend. Other animals have gone to her, even the tapir, the vulture, the cutia but, somehow, they never learn the name of the magic tree."

"Why is that? Won't she tell them the name?" asked Jabotí.

"Yes, indeed. The great god Tupana has commanded her to tell the name to anyone who asks for it, but nobody ever seems to remember it," explained Macaco, the monkey.

"Well, I'll see what I can do," said Jabotí firmly.

"I wish you luck, Jabotí," said the monkey, "but I'm afraid you won't do any better than the others."

Jabotí left the monkey and hurried through the forest. Not far from the house of Curica, the green parrot, he heard voices. Quickly he hid among the leaves and listened.

At the door were the parrot and Yareté, the young jaguar. Jabotí listened hard and heard the parrot say, "The name of the magic tree is Boyoyó, Boyoyó, Kizáma, Kizú——Boyoyó, Boyoyó, Kizáma, Kizú."

The jaguar thanked Curica, the green parrot, and

turned to go, but no sooner had he taken a few steps than Curica called to him.

"Yareté," she yelled. "That isn't the name at all. The name is Kimbombó, Kimbombá, Yoyó."

The young jaguar was puzzled. "That isn't the name you gave me a minute ago."

"Well, I made a mistake," said the tricky parrot. "The name isn't Kusúma, Kutíma, Kissá. It's Kimbímba, Bombímba, Rará."

The poor jaguar was so mixed up, he couldn't remember a thing.

Jabotí knew now what kind of a trick the parrot played. He understood why the animals couldn't remember the name of the magic tree. He made up his mind she wouldn't play the same trick on him. Instead, he would play a better one on her. So he took his flute and knocked at the door. Curica, the green parrot, opened it.

"Good morning," said Jabotí politely. "Will you please tell me the name of that tree over there?"

The parrot said angrily. "I've told that name to every animal in this forest. Can I help it if you are all so stupid you forget everything!"

"Please," begged Jabotí, "tell it to me just once."

"Very well," she finally agreed. "I'll tell it to

you just once, but if you forget it, don't come again
—and don't send anyone else!''

Then she called out very fast, "The name is
Boyoyó, Boyoyó, Kizáma, Kizú——Boyoyó, Boyoyó, Kizáma, Kizú.''

"Oh, please, senhora Curica, please repeat it once
more. I don't hear very well.''

"If he is deaf," thought the parrot, "it won't do any
harm to repeat it.'' Aloud she said, "Boyoyó, Boyoyó,
Kizáma, Kizú——Boyoyó, Boyoyó, Kizáma, Kizú.''

Jabotí said the name over and over again to himself to be sure he knew it. Then he waved good-
bye to the parrot, thanked her politely, and started
for the tree.

He had taken only a few steps when the parrot
called out to him as she had done to the others. "Oh,
friend Jabotí," she shouted. "That wasn't the name
of the magic tree. The name is . . ." but before she
could say anymore, Jabotí had taken out his flute

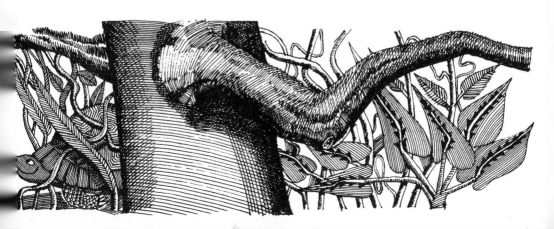

and was playing music as loud as he could. The parrot tried and tried to mix him up but Jabotí couldn't hear a thing she said. His flute drowned her voice. All he could hear was the music and the words Boyoyó, Boyoyó, Kizáma, Kizú, which he kept repeating to himself over and over again.

When he reached the magic tree, he was surprised to find the young jaguar waiting for him. "What are you doing here, Yareté?" he asked.

"I saw you go to Curica, the green parrot, to learn the name of the magic tree," said Yareté. "I thought I'd wait and find out how you made out, Jabotí. Tell me what happened. Did you learn the name of the magic tree?"

"Of course I learned the name of the magic tree. Did you think I'd fail? The trouble with all of you was that you allowed that green parrot to trick you. But she didn't trick me."

Yareté didn't know whether to believe Jabotí or not. At last, he said, "If you really know the name of the magic tree, why don't you say it?"

"Because I am waiting for you to go home. As soon as I get some fruit, you'll take it from me."

"No, I won't. Oh please, Jabotí. Don't be selfish.

I promise not to take the fruit from you. All I want
is to taste it."

Jabotí wasn't at all sure that was all the jaguar
wanted but he finally agreed. "Here's the name,"
he said. Then clearly, out loud, he uttered the words
he had learned. "Boyoyó, Boyoyó. Kizáma, Kizú
——Boyoyó, Boyoyó, Kizáma, Kizú."

They waited and waited but no fruit fell to the
ground.

"I knew it," said Yareté. "You don't know the
name at all. See, the fruit is still on the tree."

"Do you expect it to come down of its own
accord?" asked Jabotí, peeved. "Someone will have
to go up after it."

The young jaguar was pleased. He was pleased

because he knew Jabotí couldn't climb trees. "Since you can't climb, Jabotí," he said, "I'll go up after the fruit."

"Very well," agreed Jabotí. "Bring the fruit to me and I'll give you some for helping me."

The jaguar picked up his bag and climbed the magic tree. Then he began to eat. He ate and ate and ate until there wasn't much left for anybody.

From the ground, Jabotí could see what Yareté was doing. He was furious but he said nothing.

When the jaguar couldn't eat anymore, he put what was left in his bag and came down.

"Yareté," snapped Jabotí, "you're selfish. You ate nearly all the fruit. Now give me what is in the bag."

Yareté laughed. "Did you really think I'd be foolish enough to give you the fruit?" he said. "Indeed not! Now you'll have to wait for a whole year before the fruit ripens again." He picked up the bag and put it on his back.

Poor Jabotí was so angry and disappointed he could have cried but he didn't show Yareté how he felt. Instead he pretended to be friendly. "You win, Yareté. You're stronger than I. I can't fight you." Then he asked, "May I walk with you a little way?"

"You may if you want to," answered the jaguar pleased with himself. "But don't expect me to give you any fruit because I won't." They went off side by side.

When they came to a small river, Jabotí said sweetly, "Friend Yareté, I am a better swimmer than you are. If you'll promise to give me one or two fruits, I'll carry your bag to the other side of the river. I'll wait for you on the opposite bank."

The jaguar agreed quickly because he knew he couldn't carry the bag and swim at the same time. He still had no intention of giving fruit to Jabotí, even though he had promised. What could little Jabotí do about it, anyway?

Jabotí took the bag and swam to the other side of the river as fast as he could go. He came up on the opposite bank not far from one of his many holes in the ground. Quick as a flash he disappeared into a hole taking the bag with him.

From the river, Yareté saw Jabotí plunge into a hole but he couldn't see exactly where he went. When he finally reached the bank, he looked around. He looked here, there, everywhere, but he could not see Jabotí nor the hole. Disgusted, he sat down under a tree near the spot where he had last seen the

"What's the matter with you, Yareté? Have you gone crazy?" asked the amused monkey.

"Not at all, friend Macaco. Would you believe it, my tail has taken to answering me back when I speak?"

"Is that so? Well, well, well," said the monkey chuckling to himself.

"Yes, it's terrible. I don't know what to do. Please, friend Macaco, do something for me."

The monkey didn't like the jaguar very much but he said, "All right. What do you want me to do?"

"I want you to give my tail a good whipping. It must be punished for being so impudent."

Jabotí peeped through the hole in the ground to see what was happening. He wanted to laugh out loud at the stupid jaguar but he didn't dare.

The monkey was thinking. "What a stupid fellow this jaguar is! But I'll be delighted to do what he asks."

He took a thick switch and began to spank the jaguar's tail. He spanked and spanked and spanked, until the jaguar howled with pain.

"That's enough! That's enough, friend Macaco. I can't stand anymore," pleaded Yareté, at last.

The monkey stopped whipping the tail and

tortoise. His tail rested right over the hole but Yareté didn't know it. He called out, "Jabotí, Jabotí, where are you?"

Jabotí answered from inside of the hole, "Oy."

The jaguar looked back but he couldn't see Jabotí. He called again, "Jabotí, Jabotí." Again the answer, "Oy," came from the place where his tail rested. The stupid jaguar thought it was his tail answering. He tried again, "Jabotí, Jabotí," he called. Again the answer, "Oy," came from his tail. He was scared and angry.

"Just you keep quiet, tail," he ordered sternly. "I'm not talking to you." But again the tail answered, "Oy."

The young jaguar was furious. "Imagine my own tail answering me back! This won't do at all. I'll have to punish it, but how?"

He thought, "I'll run after my tail and catch it and then I'll punish it." He started running after his tail. Around and around he went. Now he almost had it—now it was gone. He kept running around and around until he was so dizzy he could scarcely stand up.

While he was going through these funny motions, Macaco, the monkey, passed by.

quickly scurried up a tree, afraid the jaguar might decide to punish him.

Yareté, the jaguar, went away, sulking.

Jabotí was satisfied. He had the fruit and his enemy had a lashing.

The Tapir Buries Jabotí

7 It was breakfast time on the Amazon. The birds were busy eating their worms. The butterflies were sipping the honey from the flowers. The monkeys were eating the tender flesh of the young coconuts. Even the boa constrictor, who ate once in every month, was enjoying his breakfast of fresh young frogs.

Jabotí, the tortoise, was having the best breakfast of all. He was under the inajá palm tree feasting on a large cluster of ripe fruit that the wind had blown down during the night.

"What a delicious breakfast all to myself," he said as he bit into the fruit and felt the juice drip from the corners of his mouth. "Lucky for me that Tapira, the tapir, overslept this morning."

No sooner had he spoken than a deep voice thundered in his ear, a voice so gruff it made him tremble all over.

"Get out of my way, Jabotí. That's my breakfast you're eating."

It was the tapir.

"Your breakfast?" snapped Jabotí. "What are you saying? I got here first. It's my breakfast."

"I don't care who got here first. I want that fruit. So get out of my way," said Tapira who was a nasty creature.

"I won't go," said Jabotí flatly.

"You had better go or I'll step on you. You know I'm heavy and if I step on you, you'll sink into the ground and never come out."

"You're not heavy enough for that. It would take you and three animals like you to tread me into the ground," said Jabotí bravely though he was scared to death.

"Come on now, don't talk so much, but just get away from that fruit."

"I won't budge for you or anybody," insisted Jabotí.

"I give you one last warning. Are you going, or shall I step on you?"

"I'm not afraid of you," said Jabotí. "I won't give up my breakfast for you."

"We'll see," the tapir said roughly. He stepped

forward and put his large foot down, smack down on the tortoise's back. Jabotí sank deep, deep into the ground until he was completely buried in the dirt and could not move. It was the dry season and the ground was hard so that poor Jabotí was caught fast and held down as if he had been glued to the spot.

He tried and tried to free himself but all he succeeded in doing was getting his nose above the ground so he could breathe.

"Ha, ha, ha," laughed the cruel tapir. "You made a mistake when you defied me. Now you can stay here until doomsday for all I care." He bent his head and ate the rest of Jabotí's breakfast while the tortoise looked on hungrily.

Jabotí sighed, "You win this time, you selfish creature. But wait until the rainy season. The ground will be soft then and I'll be able to get away from here. Then you'd better look out for I'll get even with you."

"A little worm like you can't frighten me," said Tapira.

After he had eaten all of the fruit, he went off chuckling to himself leaving the unhappy tortoise buried with only his nose above ground.

Jabotí stuck fast to the ground for one week, for two weeks, for three weeks, for . . . he didn't know how many weeks. And still it didn't rain. He looked constantly at the sky hoping to see the clouds gather, but it was as bright and clear as a midsummer's day.

"Oh, great god Tupana," he prayed, "let the rains come early this year. I must get away from here and punish Tapira for the way he has treated me."

But no rain came.

At last, when poor Jabotí was so hungry and so stiff he didn't know how much longer he could stand it, it began to rain. At first only a few drops

fell, then more and more, until finally there came a terrific downpour such as sometimes occurs on the Amazon.

Jabotí could feel the water seeping into the earth. He was glad. Slowly, but surely, it began to loosen up the earth about him. He waited until the ground was soft enough before he tried to move. He moved one foot. He moved another foot. Then he moved the third foot . . . then the fourth foot and . . . lo and behold, he was free.

Though he was free, he was so stiff he could scarcely walk. He drank water from a nearby puddle made by the rain and fell fast asleep, sleeping the first sound sleep he had had in a long, long time.

When he awoke, the rain had stopped. The clouds had disappeared from the sky, and the sun was shining brightly on the fresh, green grass.

Jabotí took a deep breath and drank in the strange fragrance of the jungle. He was refreshed and rested. "Now," he said to himself, "I shall set out to find that nasty Tapira and when I find him, I'll make him sorry he ever stepped on me."

At once he set out asking everyone he met, "Do you know where Tapira is?"

No one knew. He asked the monkeys. They didn't know. He asked the jaguar. He didn't know. He asked the boa constrictor. He didn't know. Nobody knew where the tapir had gone.

Jabotí walked and walked for many hours. He walked and walked for many days. Still he could not find Tapira. He walked and walked, stopping only long enough to eat and drink, asking the same question, "Do you know where I can find Tapira?"

Everyone gave him the same answer, "I don't know."

At last he asked Urubú, the vulture, if he knew where he could find Tapira.

"Why do you want to know where Tapira is? Do you want him to step on you a second time?" asked the vulture.

"I wasn't born to be a stone and live in the ground," snapped Jabotí. "Tell me, if you know. Where is Tapira?"

"I'm not going to tell you where he is. Besides, he is fast asleep and shouldn't be disturbed."

"Thank you very much, Urubú," said Jabotí. "If he is asleep, I know where to find him."

He went off leaving the surprised vulture gasping.

Jabotí went directly to the spot where he knew he would find Tapira. There, in a thicket of ferns, he found Tapira fast asleep.

Jabotí was puzzled. "Now that I have found him, how am I going to punish him?" He thought and thought. "I can't bury him. He is so strong he would soon free himself, especially now that the ground is wet. I don't want to hurt him. I know what I'll do. I'll tie his feet together with a stout vine. Then he'll have to stay here until someone unties him. They won't find him easily. This place is not easy to find. Yes, that's what I'll do. I'll tie him and then he'll know what it is like to suffer hunger and thirst, as I did."

He took a strong vine and tied the tapir's hind legs together, being careful not to waken him. But he need not have worried. Tapira is a heavy sleeper and doesn't waken easily. Jabotí took another vine and tied his front legs together. Then he left him and went away.

When Tapira awoke and found himself tied, he was furious. He roared and roared, screamed and grunted, threatened and coaxed, but there was no one there to hear him. He was alone. Later, birds and ants passed that way but they would not help him.

"He is getting just what he deserves," they said. "He has been cruel to our kind friend, Jabotí."

Tapira stayed tied in that position for one day, for two days, for three days. He was so hungry and so thirsty that he thought he was going to die. Instead of roaring, he began to whine and to plead with the birds, with the ants, but no one would help him.

Finally, Jabotí himself felt sorry for Tapira. He knew he couldn't go much longer without food and water. "He's been punished enough," the tortoise said to himself. "Tapira knows now what it is to go hungry and thirsty. I hope it'll be a lesson to him."

He went to Tapira's father who lived at another part of the jungle. "Mr. Tapir," he said. "I think something terrible has happened to your son, Tapira. I heard him moaning in that mass of ferns at the far end of the jungle. Maybe you had better go there and see what is the matter."

Tapira's father thanked Jabotí. "I have missed him for several days and wondered where he could be," he said.

"I think he is in serious trouble, so you better

hurry if you want to save him," urged the good-hearted tortoise.

So Tapira's father set out to find his son. And if he hadn't found him and freed him, Tapira would be there yet.

Jabotí
Takes a Tumble

8 It was early morning on the Amazon. The toads climbed to the tops of the trees to look at the sun. The monkeys climbed. The snakes climbed. The lizards climbed. Even the vines and palms stretched their long necks to feel the magic warmth of the tropical sun.

Jabotí, the tortoise, raised his head. All he could see was a sea of leaves out of which sprang trees and vines. All he could smell was the sickening smell of crushed plants, the whiffs of decaying wood and the oversweet smell of vanilla.

"How sad it is," he muttered aloud, "that I should be such a little fellow. I can hardly get my head above the leaves. All I see are leaves and more leaves. I almost have to break my neck to see the top of a tree and a bit of the sky. And if I want to see the sun, I have to walk a long way over to the banks of the river." He sighed deeply. "How I wish I were a bird and could travel beyond the clouds!"

Urubú, the vulture, heard Jabotí muttering to himself. "What's the matter, Jabotí?" he asked. "Why are you grumbling?"

"Oh, I'm just tired of seeing nothing but trees and dead leaves and underbrush. I'd like to be a bird and fly up, up to the sky."

"Do you really think you'd like to go up above the clouds?" asked Urubú.

"Oh, yes indeed," answered Jabotí quickly.

"Well, listen. The great god Tupana has called a meeting of all the birds of the Amazon forests. He holds his court on a cloud, high up in the sky. I'll take you with me if you care to go."

"Will you really?" asked Jabotí all excited.

"Sure, I will."

"Oh, I'll be so happy. I'll . . . I'll never be able to thank you enough, friend Urubú."

"I'll take you with me but you may be sorry."

"I won't be sorry. I'm sure I won't be sorry," insisted Jabotí.

"Get ready, then," he said. "Tomorrow, when the sun is directly over that large palm tree, I'll come for you."

"How will you carry me?"

"On my back. You climb up my back and hang on to my feathers."

"What if I fall?"

"You won't fall. I'll be careful and fly very smoothly without moving my wings too much."

"All right," agreed Jabotí. "I'll be here."

When the vulture had gone, Jabotí felt himself getting weak all over. He looked up. Two vultures were flying about in the sky. They were going up, up, up, until they were tiny specks in the blue. Finally he couldn't see them at all. Jabotí's knees trembled. The great height, the awful distance frightened him. He would have liked to take back his promise but he didn't want the vulture to know he was afraid. Oh, no, not Jabotí! *He* wasn't afraid of anything or anybody!

Jabotí was really worried this time.

The next day dawned bright and sunny. The sky was so clear it looked like an ocean of blue. Jabotí went to the place where he had promised to meet Urubú. He was hoping that the vulture had changed his mind about taking him. Maybe he wouldn't come but . . . no, there on the tree above him was Urubú.

"Hello, Jabotí," he greeted. "Are you ready?"

"Of course, I am, Urubú, all ready," said Jabotí gaily.

"Aren't you afraid?"

"No, indeed. Why should I be afraid?"

"Very well," said Urubú as he flew down to the ground. "You climb up my back and hold tight. I'll carry you up to the sky, and then you'll meet the great god Tupana face to face."

Slowly and carefully Jabotí climbed up the vulture's back and took a firm grip on his feathers, but he didn't like the position he was in at all. He said, "Urubú, do you really think I'll be safe here?"

The vulture answered, "Oh, yes, you'll be as safe on my back as you are on the ground."

Jabotí had his doubts but he said nothing.

Poor Jabotí could feel his heart beat . . . pit-a-pat . . . pit-a-pat . . . pit-a-pat as the vulture took off slowly and gracefully over the river. He flew up, up, up. Jabotí was afraid to look down. All he could do was to hold on tightly.

Jabotí was too frightened to enjoy the beauties and wonders he had been so anxious to see. They passed two araras with brilliant feathers. These birds greeted Jabotí but he didn't answer.

Jabotí was afraid. For the first time in his life he

was really afraid. He had never been so afraid, not even when the tapir stepped on him and buried him in the hard earth. Why did he wish to fly like the birds? Why wasn't he satisfied to stay on earth? At this moment he wanted nothing better than to feel the friendly ground underneath his feet.

"Oh, Urubú," he called at last. "Please, please take me down. I'm getting dizzy."

The vulture said, "Don't be afraid. If you are as brave as you pretend to be, you'll go with me all the way up."

"I'm . . . I'm not afraid, Urubú," said Jabotí but his jaws chattered.

"If you're not afraid, look down. See what a tiny speck the jungle is now."

"I can't look down. I'm afraid to look down."

"Do you admit at last that you're afraid?" laughed Urubú as he went higher and higher.

"I'm not exactly afraid," stuttered the tortoise. "It's just that it's so high. I'm not used to it."

"Take one little peep," coaxed the wicked vulture.

Jabotí took one look, just one teeny, weeny look. Then everything went black. A queer feeling crept over him. He got dizzy . . . dizzy . . . dizzy . . . dizzier and dizzier until he didn't know what he was doing. He closed his eyes tightly, but it did no good. He was dizzier than ever. Gradually, gradually, he lost his hold on Urubú's feathers and felt himself slipping . . . slipping . . . slipping. Down, down he went, at terrific speed, passing clouds, birds, treetops in one confused jumble. Down, down he came, hitting the ground with a crash so hard that his shells and his body broke into little pieces.

Poor Jabotí! He lay on the ground all broken up. He would never be the same again. He was certain he was going to die.

Meanwhile, Urubú arrived at the meeting before the great god Tupana. Tupana stood tall and straight in the middle of a fleecy cloud. Around him were all the birds of the Amazon jungle. When he saw the vulture, he gave a command, "Urubú, come here," he said. "Stand before me!"

The vulture hurried to obey Tupana. "Where is Jabotí?" asked Tupana sternly.

Urubú didn't answer.

"Where is Jabotí?" repeated Tupana.

"I don't know. He must be in the jungle. At least I . . . think so," answered Urubú a little frightened.

"You know exactly where he is and what has happened to him. I saw what you did. You started to bring him here and then you let him fall."

"He deserved it for being so curious," said the wicked vulture.

"He deserved nothing of the sort," thundered the great god Tupana. "He is a very fine creature. I wish all the other animals in the jungle were as good as Jabotí. What he did was natural. At some time or another everybody wishes he were somebody else." Then he commanded, "Go down to earth this minute, all of you. Go down and do as I tell you, or Jabotí will die."

A hush fell over the birds.

"He mustn't die," they said at last. "He mustn't die. Do tell us how we can save him."

The birds fluttered about Tupana eagerly waiting for him to tell them what to do.

"Here, take this glue that I give you. It is magic. Go down to Jabotí. Urubú will show you where he is. Pick up the pieces and patch him up. See that you glue him together properly. If you make any mistake, I will punish you all."

The birds saluted Tupana, took the glue, and flew down to earth. They found Jabotí where he had fallen. There was scarcely any breath left in his body.

"How sad," said the Japím bird tearfully.

"What a pity," said the parrots.

"Be careful," went on the Japím bird who had taken charge of the mending. "Pick up the pieces carefully and let us put Jabotí together as Tupana ordered."

The first birds that picked up Jabotí afterward had spotted feathers. Others turned red. Those that glued the shells together got black beaks. Those that worked on the liver turned green.

At last Jabotí was as good as new except that now he had shells patched together instead of in one piece as they used to be.

Never again did Jabotí wish he were a bird or could travel above the clouds.

The Jaguar
Steals Jabotí's Flute

9   Jabotí, the tortoise, was angry. He was angry enough to eat stones. He was so angry he wished he were the great god Tupana so he could send down a rainstorm that would destroy the world.

Yareté, the jaguar, had stolen his flute!

Jabotí without his flute was like a firefly without light, like an elephant without his trunk, like a bee without honey . . . like . . . like . . . like the night without stars, the world without the sun.

For three days he walked up and down, up and down the banks of the Amazon trying to decide how to get back his flute. For two nights he didn't sleep. It wasn't until the end of the third day that he worked out a plan. After that he slept soundly.

The next morning, bright and early, he set out to find Yareté, the jaguar. As soon as he saw the jaguar, he began to run. He ran and he ran, panting all the time. He panted and he ran as if he had been running for a long time.

"What's the matter, Jabotí?" asked Yareté curiously. "Why are you running so fast?"

"Haven't you heard? There's a storm coming, a storm so great it will carry away all the animals."

"No, I haven't heard anything about it. Even if a storm is coming, what good will it do you to run?"

"Do you expect me to stay here and be blown away? Not I. I'm going to my hole where I'll be safe."

Yareté was worried.

"Wait a minute," he begged. "What is to become of me?"

"How do I know? I know what *I'm* going to do. Now it's up to you to decide what *you're* going to do."

"If I were tied to that large tree, do you think I'd be safe?"

"I don't know. You might be. But who is going to tie you?"

"You are, Jabotí."

"I haven't time."

"Please, please, Jabotí, tie me," begged Yareté.

"Tie me or I'll be blown away. I'm so big the wind will carry me away first. Do tie me before it's too late."

Jabotí laughed within himself. His plan was working out better than he had expected. Imagine the jaguar asking to be tied! Not only asking but begging to be tied! And Jabotí did tie him. He took a thick vine and tied him so securely no one could untie him without a great deal of trouble. Then he went off saying, "Good-bye, Yareté. I'll see you tomorrow. When I come, you'd better have my flute or I'll keep you tied until doomsday."

Yareté was scared to death. "Don't leave me, Jabotí!" he begged. "Come back, Jabotí, come back!" But Jabotí was gone and Yareté knew he had been tricked again.

Yareté roared and groaned, groaned and roared until his voice was hoarse, but no one came to free him. No one passed that way, not that day, nor that night, nor the following morning. It wasn't until late in the afternoon of the second day that help came to him.

A tiny white ant passed by, carrying a leaf many times larger than himself. The jaguar didn't expect much help from an ant but he called to him just the same. "Maybe," he thought, "maybe he will take a message to my father."

"Oh, Copím," he called. "Oh, good, kind Copím. Will you please do an errand for me?"

The white ant looked up. He was surprised to see the king of the jungle tied to a tree. "Who could have tied you like this? It must have been some strange, strong animal that did this to you," said the puzzled Copím.

"No, it wasn't. It was Jabotí."

"Jabotí? Do you mean to say that that tiny tortoise tied you to a tree? My . . . my!"

"Yes, he did," said the tired Yareté. "But it was a trick . . . a trick, do you understand? I'll make him pay dearly for this, see if I don't. I can't explain now . . . I'm too weak . . . but please, Copím, run to my father and ask him to come here and untie me."

"We won't have to call your father, Yareté," said the kindhearted white ant. "Let me help you."

"You? What can you do?"

"Wait and see."

Copím hurried away while Yareté fumed and

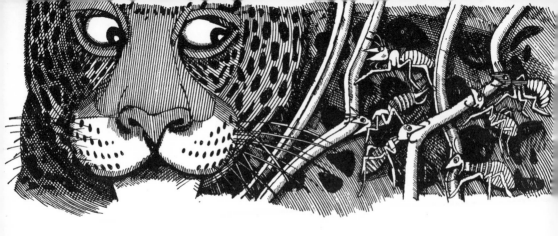

fretted and whined . . . yes, whined like a puppy. He was so tired he could have cried.

In a little while Copím, the white ant, came back. He was not alone. With him were a number of his brother ants. They set to work gnawing and chewing at the vine that bound Yareté to the tree.

Meanwhile, Jabotí returned to the place where he had left Yareté, to see what had happened to his prisoner. He hid behind a bush just as Yareté was saying to the white ant, "Oh, Copím, I don't know how to thank you. But anytime you care to visit me, do so. I'll treat you well. I'll give you the best food and the driest place to sleep in. Do come to see me."

"I'm usually too busy to go visiting, but I'll try. Thank you just the same." Copím and the other white ants went back to their work of carrying leaves and twigs.

Jabotí was disappointed. After going to all that

trouble, he didn't get back his flute. What should he do? He decided to try again. He knew where to find some honey, so he went there and rolled in the honey until he was sticky all over. Then he went to the nest of the white ants, shook a number of them to the ground, and rolled among them. The white ants stuck fast to the honey, like flies to flypaper.

With white ants sticking all over him, Jabotí looked like something the white ants had made. He went to the house of the jaguar. When the jaguar saw him, he ran to tell his father. "Father," he said excitedly, "here comes the king of the white ants. You remember, the white ants saved my life the other day when that bad Jabotí tied me? I told Copím to be sure to visit me, but he sent the king instead. He must be a great king, too. Look how many white ants he has on his body."

Yareté's father hurried to meet the king of the white ants. He didn't know it was Jabotí in disguise. Had he known who it was, there wouldn't have been very much left of Jabotí.

Jabotí, himself, was nervous. What if Yareté should find out who he really was? What if his trick didn't work? His knees shook but he greeted Yareté and his father bravely. "How do you do, Yareté? How do you do, Mr. Jaguar? You see, the white ants have sent me to visit you."

"Come right in. Come right in, Your Majesty. We are privileged by your visit."

Jabotí was ushered in with all ceremony. Yareté and his father rushed here and there to prepare the best dinner possible for their visitor—the visitor they thought was the king of the white ants.

When he was inside, Jabotí's eyes looked here, looked there, looked everywhere, but they couldn't see any sign of the flute.

After dinner, they sat in the moonlight and chatted. Suddenly, Jabotí gave a deep sigh. "It's such a lovely night," he sighed. "The moon is so bright. The leaves are so fresh. It would be nice to have some music. Do you play, Yareté?"

"A little. I'm just learning."

Jabotí's heart beat fast. He was all excited. "Do play for us," he coaxed.

"I don't play very well," said Yareté, but he went inside and brought out the flute . . . Jabotí's flute! Jabotí had tried and tried but he couldn't see where the flute had been hidden.

Yareté put the flute to his lips and played, but the

sounds he made were terrible. He held the flute this way, he held it that way, but always the sounds that came out were dreadful.

Jabotí listened politely but his fingers ached to hold his beloved flute. "I didn't know you played the flute, Yareté," said Jabotí innocently when the jaguar had finished. "I thought Jabotí, the tortoise, was the only one who played the flute."

"Yes, he is," agreed Yareté. "In fact this is Jabotí's flute. I took it from him."

"Didn't Jabotí ever try to get his flute back?"

"Yes, he did. But what can that undersized creature do against me, a jaguar?"

Jabotí said no more.

Soon, clouds gathered in the sky and covered the moon. Yareté's father said, "I believe it's going to rain. We had better go to bed."

Hoping to see where Yareté would put the flute, Jabotí was the first to enter the house. He followed every move closely. Finally, he saw Yareté put the flute behind a chair. Jabotí gave a sigh of relief. At last he knew where his flute was. Now he must wait for a chance to take it.

Yareté's father gave Jabotí the best place to sleep in. They said good night to each other, then took their places in separate corners just as Yareté's father told them to.

Jabotí pretended to be asleep, but he kept one eye open. He waited and waited but nothing happened. At last he heard Yareté snore. Then he heard Yareté's father snore. Now was the time to do something!

He slipped out of bed quietly, tiptoed to the place where he had seen Yareté put the flute, and reached out to grab it. Slowly, slowly, trying not to breathe, he pulled the flute from its hiding place and held it close to his body.

With the flute in his hand, he started for the door. In his haste, he stumbled over a chair. He was afraid to breathe. Yareté moved in his sleep. Jabotí nearly fainted.

He took another step and stopped . . . Yareté's father moved, too. Jabotí's heart almost stopped beating. He was scared to death. He lay quiet, quiet as a mouse until the snoring began again. Then he made a dash for the door and ran, helter-skelter, for one of his nearest holes.

By this time, rain began to fall in torrents the way it does in the Amazon. Yareté's father awoke. "Yareté," he called to his son. "See if the king is comfortable. I gave him a dry place to sleep in but you never can tell what may have happened. There could be a leak in the roof."

Yareté went to the corner where Jabotí had been sleeping. Jabotí wasn't there! "Father, Father," he called wildly. "Come quickly. The king of the white ants is gone."

All excited, Yareté's father jumped to his feet. "What could have happened to the king? Let us go out and look for him."

"It's raining too hard," said Yareté.

"No matter. We must see to it that nothing has happened to our important visitor."

Just as they were about to go out into the pouring rain, they heard a flute playing in the distance, followed by Jabotí's voice singing gaily:

Oh, my flute, my flute, my beloved flute
Yareté isn't going to have you anymore.

Yareté and his father looked at each other in surprise.

"What do you think of that?" exclaimed Yareté. "It wasn't the king of the white ants at all. It was Jabotí!"

At last Jabotí had his flute. He wasn't angry anymore.

Turtle Soup

10 Jabotí, the tortoise, was tired of the jungle. He was tired of living in the same place all the time. He was tired of ferns, of palms, of the dense underbrush. He was tired of fighting with the tapir, the jaguar, the alligator. He was even tired of seeing the same birds, beautiful though they were. He was so tired he decided to go far, far away to lands the vulture told him about, to lands where a strange creature, called man, lived. So one bright morning he set out on his travels, taking with him only his flute.

He walked for days. He walked for weeks. He walked for months, but no man did he see.

"I wonder where man lives," he muttered to himself.

Suddenly one morning he found himself out of the woods and in a large field covered with grass.

In the field were many strange animals, animals Jabotí had never seen before.

"Good morning," he said politely to the one who seemed to be the leader. "Do you mind if I cross this field?"

"Not at all," answered the big fellow cheerfully. "Help yourself to the grass. There's plenty here for everybody."

"Thank you," said Jabotí, "but I'm not hungry." Then he asked, "Will you please tell me your name? I've never seen animals like you before."

"Haven't you? That's queer. There are a great many like us in the world. I'm Mr. Bull and this is Mrs. Cow. The others out there are all cows. We belong to a mighty creature called man."

"How do you do?" said Jabotí to Mrs. Cow. Then he turned to Mr. Bull. "Does man feed you? He must be very kind."

"He's not as kind as you think. He feeds us because the cows give milk. And man likes milk very much. But tell me, where are you going?"

"I'm going to see the world. I want to see this *man*, as he is called. Will you tell me what he is like?"

"Just listen to this, Mrs. Cow. Here's a creature

who has never seen man." Then he explained to Jabotí, "Man is different from anything you have ever seen. He is very wise and very, very clever. He stands erect and has two hands and two feet."

"Is he as strong as the jaguar?" inquired Jabotí curiously.

"No, indeed. He's not strong at all, but he could easily kill the jaguar."

"How can that be if, as you say, he isn't strong?"

"He does it with a funny thing that he makes himself. It spurts out fire from its nose and anyone in front of it dies. Besides. . . ." He stopped suddenly. "Dear me, here he comes. He mustn't see us talking together. He doesn't want us to talk to strangers."

Jabotí looked up. There before him was the queerest creature he had ever seen. He was tall, taller than a fern, and he stood up straighter than a monkey. He had no hair on his face, but wore something soft and clinging on his chest and legs. Jabotí stared and stared.

The man looked at Jabotí and knew him at once. "Tortoise, come here!" he commanded sternly.

Jabotí was afraid of him but he dared not disobey that voice. Slowly he went to the man.

"What luck!" said the man laughing. "Turtle soup for my supper!" and he smacked his lips.

Jabotí shivered. He was too scared to move.

The man stooped and picked him up easily, holding him by the back so he couldn't snap if he wanted to. Poor Jabotí was so frightened he couldn't think about anything except what was going to happen to him.

Then and there, Jabotí decided he would never again want to be a bird or a monkey, nor would he want to see the world. After this, he would be satisfied with being a tortoise and living in the Amazon jungle.

The man took him to a huge house surrounded by trees. Inside, he saw many things he had never seen before: arrows and guns, spears and chairs, table and hammocks. Of course, Jabotí didn't know what they were. Soon the man put him in a box and all he could see was a bit of the ceiling covered with palm leaves.

In the house, also, were two creatures just like man but much smaller. They called the man "Papá" which, as you know, means "Daddy." The man said to them, "Children, we're going to have this tortoise for supper. I have to go out now, so you stay here and watch him. Don't let him get away." So saying, the man went out.

Poor Jabotí was frantic. Here at last was the end of his days. Such a miserable way to die! What had he done to die in a soup pot? If he could only think of some way to free himself! He knew how to play tricks on other animals, but this creature, man, was a mystery to him. He didn't like it at all.

When Jabotí was happy, he played his flute. When he was sad, he played his flute. Now that he was about to die, he would also play his flute. So he took out his beloved flute and played.

The children heard him and went closer to the box. Jabotí stopped playing, thinking they wouldn't like it. He was surprised when they said, "Go on playing, tortoise. We like it. You play very well."

Jabotí was pleased. "Do you really like it?"

"Yes, we like it very much."

"Very well, I'll play some more. I'm going to die, anyway. I might just as well die happy. But first tell me: Who are you?"

"We are two little boys named Joaquím and José. The man who caught you is our father."

Jabotí played a tune that was very sad.

Joaquím said to his brother, "Isn't it a pity to have

to kill a tortoise that plays such beautiful music?"

José agreed. "It's too bad, but we must obey Papai."

Jabotí heard what they said and began to see a ray of hope. Maybe . . . maybe, if he tried . . . he could get away. The little boys were not so clever as the big man. He would try, anyway. Oh, if he could only think of one of the tricks for which he was so famous. He needed to think of some plan now, more than ever.

"You should see me dance," he said at last.

"Do you dance, too?" marvelled the boys.

"Indeed I do. I dance very well, even if I say so myself. Why, in the jungle where I live—oh, how he wished he were there right now—I'm the champion dancer. I know all the latest steps. If you'll let me out of here for a few minutes, I'll show you a dance I invented. It's called the Jabotí Walk."

"How can you think of dancing when you're going to die?"

"Oh, well, I might just as well die while playing and dancing, as die while crying. If I'm going to die, I'm going to die, and that's all there is to it."

The boys talked it over between them and decided to let the tortoise out of the box for a few minutes. "Only for a few minutes, understand," they said.

When Jabotí saw himself out of the box, he heaved a sigh of relief. He had succeeded in getting out of the box. What should he do next?

José said, "Why don't you dance, tortoise? You promised to show us that new dance, the . . . what did you call it?"

"The Jabotí Walk. I dance much better in the grass than I do in the house," explained Jabotí carefully. "I'm not used to these hard floors; they hurt my feet. If you'll just let me go outside for a little while, I'll show you how well I can dance. The Jabotí Walk needs a lot of room."

Joaquím and José again talked it over and decided it wouldn't do any harm to let Jabotí dance outside. So outside they went.

Jabotí began to dance.

"How well you dance," the boys said, clapping their hands in delight.

Jabotí didn't know any such dance as the Jabotí Walk, but he tried to explain the steps to the boys. "Yes," he began slowly. He spoke slowly because he was making up the steps as he went along. "This

114

is a special kind of dance. You start in a small circle like this and then dance in a larger and larger circle. When the circle is very large, you can do the best steps because you have more room. You try it, too. You boys dance over there while I dance here."

Then he began to jump, to stoop, to turn this way and that. He bent his head forward, he bent his head backward, while he danced in an ever larger circle. He danced as if he were mad.

Joaquím and José were trying to imitate him. They were so busy learning the steps, they forgot to notice how far away Jabotí had gone. He went farther and farther away from the boys until, before they knew what had happened, he had taken a few extra steps and disappeared in the hollow of a tree. The boys didn't know where he had gone.

They didn't search for long. Soon Joaquím said, "I'm glad he has escaped, aren't you?"

José agreed. "Yes, I am, too. I couldn't eat him anyway. He's too nice. But what will Papai say when he comes home and finds the tortoise gone? He'll surely punish us. What shall we do?"

They went off and found a stone just about the size of Jabotí. They painted the stone to look like the shell of the tortoise and put it in the box where Jabotí had been a prisoner.

When the man came home that night, he asked, "Is the tortoise here?"

The children said, "Yes, he's here."

"Is the water boiling?"

"Yes, it's boiling."

"What are you waiting for, then? Put him in it at once," he ordered.

The children looked at each other. Slowly, they took the stone and put it into the water.

After it had boiled for some time, the man said,

"Take it out, now. It has cooked long enough. Bring it here to me. I'll put it on this platter and remove the shells."

So the boys took the pot with the stone in it and brought it to the table. They looked on nervously while their father took off the lid and emptied the contents of the pot into the platter. The stone fell with a bang. The dish broke. The man jumped up angrily.

"Come here," he commanded. "What has happened to the tortoise?"

"He . . . he escaped," Joaquím answered in a whisper.

"You let him escape, didn't you? Now I'm going to punish you both. Go right to bed this instant. Do you hear me? Go to bed without supper."

Just as he spoke, a sweet sound came from the darkness outside. Jabotí was playing his flute.

The man heard it and exclaimed, "That's the tortoise. He had a flute with him when I caught him. I'll catch him again. He won't escape me this time until he's in the pot."

Joaquím began to cry. "Oh, do let him go, Papai. Please. He is so nice. He danced and played for us. Punish us, but let him go."

"I want my supper. I made up my mind I was going to have turtle soup for supper and turtle soup I will have."

He went out into the darkness in search of Jabotí. He called, "Tortoise, tortoise."

Jabotí didn't answer. He knew now that the man was his enemy and he made up his mind he wouldn't be caught again.

Again the man called, "Tortoise, tortoise."

This time Jabotí answered, but he was far away from the man. The man followed the sound and called again. Again Jabotí answered, and again the answer came from a different part of the field.

This went on and on until the man was so tired he wasn't hungry anymore. All he wanted was to go home and sleep in his hammock.

That night, both he and the boys went to bed without supper and without turtle soup.

Meanwhile, Jabotí danced the Jabotí Walk in a straight line as he hurried back to the jungle where he would be safe from such a cruel creature as man.

The Return of the Wanderer

11   There was gloom in the Amazon jungle. The birds did not sing. The trees did not rustle their leaves. The bees did not buzz. The monkeys did not chatter. Even the toads failed to croak.

For Jabotí had gone away!

"Where can he have gone?" asked the butterflies all aflutter.

"I wish I knew," said the jaguar, shaking his huge head.

"It serves you right if he never comes back," scolded the birds tearfully. "You didn't treat him right. That's why he's gone away and left us forever."

"How I miss his sweet music!" put in Suasú, the deer.

"We all miss it," they exclaimed in chorus. "We all miss Jabotí, too."

"How long has he been away?" inquired the bee sadly.

"Six new moons have come and gone since he left the jungle."

"Alas, alas!"

"I don't think he'll ever come back," moaned the butterflies, fluttering their wings this way and that. "Something terrible must have happened to him. Poor Jabotí!"

"Poor Jabotí!" grunted the alligator.

"Poor Jabotí!" roared the jaguar.

"Poor Jabotí!" croaked the toad.

"Oh! oh! oh!" they all cried.

Just then, a faint sound was heard in the distance.

"Wait!" said the jaguar. "I hear something. Listen!"

They all listened closely.

Faintly at first, then louder . . . louder . . . louder . . . clearer . . . and clearer came the sound of music . . . gay, happy music.

"It's Jabotí," they chorused joyfully. "Jabotí! Jabotí!"

The birds sang. The trees rustled their leaves. The bees buzzed. The monkeys chattered. Even the toads croaked. Gloom had disappeared from the Amazon jungle.

Jabotí was home again.

Glossary

ANTEATER The Indian "Tamanduá." Has long tongue and great strength in feet. Breaks into strongest anthills with powerful claws. Extends long tongue and gathers in ants.

ARARAS Macaws. Members of parrot family of which there are many in Brazil. Have beautiful plumage and long tail. Do not sing or speak.

CURICA Green parrot readily learning how to reproduce human voice. Lives on fruit and seeds.

CUTIA A family of more or less tailless rodents. Prowls mostly by night. Lives on vegetables, fruits, and roots. In Brazilian folklore depicted as tricky and mischievous.

JABOTÍ Word "Jabotí" comes from the Tupí-Guaraní, language spoken by most of the Brazilian Indians. A tortoise with black upper and lower shells, yellow in the middle of each section of the shells. In Brazilian folklore, the Jabotí is always pictured with a flute. Credited with being wise, astute, clever—finding a solution for any problem that confronts him. The Jabotí of the fables may perhaps be the symbol or the incarnation of some wise spirit of the forests.

JAPÍM Small black and red bird. Beautiful singer as well as unusual imitator of the songs of other birds.

MACACO Word said by some to come from the Tupí, one of the two principal languages spoken by the Indians of

122

Brazil. The word usually refers to any of various old-world monkeys or lemurs, or new-world monkeys.

MANDIOCA   Plant producing basic food of Brazilians. Tuber-like roots used to make tapioca, flour, drink. Mandioca, in the form of coarse flour, is used at every meal by most of the people.

SUCURUCU   The most feared of all the poisonous snakes of Brazil.

TAPIRA   The tapir. A dark-brown mammal of great strength, sometimes attaining a length of six feet and a height of three feet. Weighs as much as five hundred pounds. Lives in jungle near rivers. When chased seeks water. Can stay under water for some time.

TUPANA   Indian god of lightning and thunder. Creator of the world and of the animals. First among the gods.

YARETÉ   (For simplicity the author has contracted "Yareté" from "Isureté"). The jaguar. A large, powerful brownish-yellow mammal, marked with black spots each of which is surrounded by a ring of somewhat smaller ones. Rules the jungle. Climbs trees. Swims rivers.

Pronunciation
of Foreign Words

ARARAS A-ra-ras
 "a" as in "art"
 Accent on "ra"
COPIM Co-pim
 "o" as in "go"
 "i" as in "sit"
 Accent on "pim"
  ("i" should have
  slight nasal sound;
  "m" should be
  sounded lightly)
CURICA Cu-ri-ca
 "u" like "oo" in "boot"
 "i" as in "sit"
 "a" as in "art"
 Accent on "ri"
CUTIA Cu-ti-a
 "u" like "oo" in "boot"
 "i" as in "sit"
 "a" as in "art"
 Accent on "ti"
GONÇALO Gon-ça-lo
 "o" as in "go"
 "a" as in "art"
 "c" like "s"
 Accent on "ca"
INAJÁ In-a-ja
 "i" as in "sit"
 "a" as in "art"
 "j" like "s" in "treasure"
 Accent on "ja"
JACARÉ Ja-ca-re
 "j" like "s" in "treasure"
 "a" as in "art"
 "e" as in "let"
 Accent on "re"
JAPÍM Ja-pim
 "j" like "s" in "treasure"
 "a" as in "art"
 "i" as in "sit"
 Accent on "pim" ("i"
  should be
  slightly nasal:
 "m" slightly sounded)
JOAQUIM Jo-a-quim
 "j" like "s" in "treasure"

"o" as in "go"
"a" as in "art"
"quim" almost
   like "keen"
Accent on "quim"
JOSÉ Jo-se
"j" like "s" in "treasure"
"o" as in "go"
"e" as in "let"
Accent on "se"
MACACO Ma-ca-co
"a" as in "art"
"o" as in "go"
Accent on "ca"
PAPAI Pa-pai
"a" as in "art"
"ae" like "y" in "my"
Accent on "ae"
SENHORA Se-nho-ra
"e" as in "let"
"nh" like middle
"n" in "onion"
"o" as in "go"

"a" as in "art"
Accent on "nho"
SUASÚ Sua-su
"sua" like
   "swa" in "swat"
"u" like "oo" in "boot"
Accent on "su"
TAPEREBA Ta-per-e-ba
"a" as in "art"
"e" as in "let"
Accent on "ba"
TAPIRA Ta-pi-ra
"a" as in "art"
"i" as in "sit"
URUBÚ U-ru-bu
"u" like "oo" in "boot"
Accent on "bu"
YARETÉ Ya-re-te
"y" as in "yet"
"a" as in "art"
"e" as in "let"
Accent on "te"